Millions of Americans remember Dick and Jane (and Sally and Spot too!). The little stories with their simple vocabulary words and warmly rendered illustrations were a hallmark of American education in the 1950s and 1960s.

But the first Dick and Jane stories actually appeared much earlier—in the Scott Foresman Elson Basic Reader Pre-Primer, copyright 1930. These books featured short, upbeat, and highly readable stories for children. The pages were filled with colorful characters and large, easy-to-read Century Schoolbook typeface. There were fun adventures around every corner of Dick and Jane's world.

Generations of American children learned to read with Dick and Jane, and many still cherish the memory of reading the simple stories on their own. Today, Pearson Scott Foresman remains committed to helping all children learn to read—and love to read. As part of Pearson Education, the world's largest educational publisher, Pearson Scott Foresman is honored to reissue these classic Dick and Jane stories, with Grosset & Dunlap, a division of Penguin Young Readers Group. Reading has always been at the heart of everything we do, and we sincerely hope that reading is an important part of your life too.

Dick and Jane is a registered trademark of Addison-Wesley Educational Publishers, Inc.
From THE NEW WE WORK AND PLAY. Copyright © 1956 by Scott, Foresman and Company,
copyright renewed 1984. From THE NEW BEFORE WE READ. Copyright © 1956 by
Scott, Foresman and Company, copyright renewed 1984. From THE NEW WE COME
AND GO. Copyright © 1956 by Scott, Foresman and Company, copyright renewed 1984.
All rights reserved. Published in 2004 by Grosset & Dunlap, a division of Penguin Young
Readers Group, 345 Hudson Street, New York, NY, 10014. GROSSET & DUNLAP is a
trademark of Penguin Group (USA) Inc. Published simultaneously in Canada. Printed in the
U.S.A.

Library of Congress Cataloging-in-Publication Data
We work.
    p. cm. — (Read with Dick and Jane ; 10)
  Summary: A collection of classic Dick and Jane stories in which they play and work with
each other, with Sally, and with their parents.
ISBN 0-448-43409-1 (pbk.) — ISBN 0-448-43495-4 (hardcover)
  [1. Play—Fiction. 2. Pets—Fiction. 3. Work—Fiction. 4. Vocabulary.] I. Series.
PZ7.W35144 2004
[E]—dc22   2003016830

ISBN 0-448-43495-4 (GB)   A B C D E F G H I J
ISBN 0-448-43409-1 (pbk)   A B C D E F G H I J

Read with
Dick and Jane

We Work

Work 5

See Sally Work 9

Funny Sally 13

Who Can Help? 17

See It Work 21

We Make Something 25

Spot Finds Something 29

GROSSET & DUNLAP • NEW YORK

Work

Work, Dick.
Work, work.

See, see.

See Dick work.

Oh, Dick.

See, see.

Oh, oh, oh.

See Sally Work

Work, work, work.
Sally can work.
See Sally work.

Oh, Dick.
Oh, Jane.
See, see.
Sally can work.

Oh, Sally.
Funny, funny Sally.
Oh, oh, oh.

Funny Sally

See Father work.

Work, work, work.

Father can work.

See Sally work.

Work, work, work.

Sally can work.

Oh, Father.

See, see.

Sally can work.

Oh, Sally.

Funny, funny Sally.

Who Can Help?

See Jane.

Jane can work.

Jane can help.

Jane can help Mother.

Jane can help Mother work.

Father can help Jane.

See It Work

Father said, "Look, Sally.

See something big.

You can see it work.

Up, up it comes.

See it work."

Sally said, "See it work.

Work, work, work."

"Help, help," said Sally.
"See my little Tim go down.
Jump down, Father.
I want my little Tim."

"Oh, Sally," said Father.
"I can not jump down.
I can not help you."

23

"Oh, see it work," said Dick.
"See it come up, up, up.
Up comes Tim to Baby Sally."

"Up, up," said Sally.
"Up comes my little Tim.
Up comes Tim to Sally."

24

We Make Something

"Look here," said Dick.
"I can make something funny.
I can make Spot.
Spot is red and blue."

"Oh, Dick," said Jane.
"I want to make something.
I want to make something blue."

"Look, Sally," said Jane.
"See my funny blue Puff.
Make something, Sally.
Make something blue."

"Oh, Jane," said Sally.
"I can not make Puff.
I can not make Spot.
I want to make little Tim."

"See me work," said Sally.
"I can make something blue.
See my funny blue Tim."

"Look, Sally," said Jane.
"Here is something for Tim.
Here is a funny red mother.
And a funny blue father.
A father and mother for Tim."

Spot Finds Something

Dick said, "Come and work.
Come and help me.
I can not find the two boats.
I can not find my red ball.
Where is my yellow boat?
Where is the blue boat?
Where is my little red ball?
Where, oh, where?"

Jane said, "I can work.

I can find two boats.

Here is the yellow boat.

Here is the blue boat."

Sally said, "I can find cars.

See my little yellow car.

See my red car and my blue car.

Where is the red ball?

Where is my little Tim?"

Dick said, "Spot can work.
Spot can find the red ball.
Spot can help me."

Sally said, "See Spot work.
Spot can find Tim.
Spot can help me."